Sir Henry, the Knight in Space

By Wendy Laing

The characters and events in this book are fictitious. Any similarity to real persons, living or dead, is coincidental and not intended by the author, except for historical references to the 'Battle of Bannockburn' 1314, King Robert the Bruce & Sir Henry de Bohun. Sir Henry and his uncle, Sir Humphrey de Bohun, the Earl of Hereford & Essex, both fought in this battle. Humphrey was made a prisoner at the battle of Bannockburn and later exchanged for Robert Bruce's wife. The story of the clash between Sir Henry and Robert Bruce is now part of the mythology & folklore of the British Isles.

Knight means simply *a boy*. As boys (like Latin *puer Cnigt.)* were used as servants, so *cnigt* came to mean a servant. Those who served the feudal kings bore arms, and persons admitted to this privilege were the king's knights; the word became a title of honour next to the nobility.

From *The Dictionary of Phrase & Fable,*

by E. Cobham Brewer.

Chapter 1
Sir Henry

Axion gasped and grabbed his twin brother Zentin's arm. The mist in the transporter dome slowly cleared and the form of someone or something appeared.

Zentin glared at Axion, then whispered hoarsely into his ear, "I told you we shouldn't have messed around with the transporter. Dad will go ballistic if he finds out!"

"Oh, he'll find out," Axion replied gloomily. "He always does."

Their father, Admiral Trebor Ecurb, was the commander of the space ship SS Ventura in which they were travelling. Admiral Trebor was also in charge of the 1,500 people recruited from Earth, who now lived at the

Space Station Explorer, in the galaxy of Starlet, wIth their families.

Axion tapped his brother's arm. "Hey, Zentin, it looks like a man in some sort of weird spacesuit! What will happen when the transporter dome lifts and releases him? We can't stop it from lifting, you know."

"Him? It looks more like an old-fashioned Roto! Although I must say, our Roto looks like a robot. But this thing looks sort of like a person. Maybe you're right, Axion. Maybe it's a man. But what if it's an alien?"

The twins clung to each other as the dome enclosing the transporter's large platform slowly rose and the thing inside started to move.

"Ooooh--My head aches!" The creature moaned and then raised its strange arm to touch what appeared to be a helmet. "Thank God, my head is still there! King Robert the Bruce actually hit me! I cannot move my helmet. It is firmly stuck. *Humph!* Ah, that is better." The metal helmet finally slipped off, revealing a human head with pale face, long wispy red hair around the sides and a large bald patch on the top. The twins were instantly intrigued by the big scar that ran from between the bushy red eyebrows over the top of the head. "Now where is that rogue Bruce? Where is my horse? Oh, God! Am I in Heaven?"

Clank! Clomp! Squeak! He moved and staggered off

the platform onto the main floor of the spaceship.

"Hello, sir," croaked Axion raising his right hand in the universal sign of salutation.

Zentin mumbled, "Welcome to the SS Ventura, sir."

"My correct name is Sir Henry de Bohun, with allegiance to King Edward the Second of England."

"King Edward the second?" replied Axion. "Sir--err, Sir Henry, there's no King of England. Or Queen, for that matter. Not for over five hundred years. They have a president. What year are you talking about?"

Sir Henry regarded them thoughtfully, then puffed out his chest. "Impudent young man, are ye not! *Humph!* I speak of King Edward II of England and the year of our Lord, 1314 AD. And what, may I ask, is a president? And pray, what is this SS Ventura that ye mentioned, lad?"

Zentin politely moved forward and held out his hand. "Welcome, Sir Henry. A president is like a king, but is elected by the people of the land. He doesn't inherit the title. You are on board the SS Ventura. This is one of the spaceships attached to the Space Station Explorer in the galaxy of Starlet."

"A space ship? Now ye are talking in riddles," replied Sir Henry.

The automatic door at the entrance of the transporter room opened silently and in hovered Roto, the spaceship robot. His staccato voice echoed around the room. "I knew I'd find you two rascals down here. Oh my, what have you done! A knight in armour?"

Sir Henry gasped, his eyes wide open. "My God, who are ye? What are ye? How did ye open that door?"

Axion interrupted. "Roto, this is Sir Henry de Bohun. I think we sort of accidentally beamed him up from the past." Axion's face flushed red.

Roto raised his right mechanical arm. "Hello, Sir Henry." He then turned and faced the boys. "The Admiral will be furious. You should not be playing with the transporter. It isn't a toy!" Roto turned back to Sir Henry. "My apologies, Sir. Welcome to the year 3000 AD, Sir Henry. My name is Roto. I fear these naughty boys have transported you up here from the past. Let me check my history data. *Hmm!* Yes! Your armour seems to be that used in the 14th century. Let me check. Helmet with *aventail* or mail skirt--breastplate-- arm defenses--gauntlets--mid sleeve chain mail--yes, all in order--made of steel with brass trim. *Hmmm.* Nice workmanship!" Roto circled around the knight, his metallic body cushioned by air jets, hovering above the ship's floor.

Sir Henry stood staring at the image of the micron- metal robot in front of him. He shook his head. "Which army do ye come from, sir? I have not seen such a suit before. It extends over thy legs right to near the floor."

Sir Henry scowled. "Show thy face from under thy helmet! Where are my soldiers? What has happened to my horse? Ooh, my head aches!" He took one more step, and then collapsed in a loud *clang*, *boing and clatter* onto the floor.

Roto turned to the twins, his arms propped against his sides. It was the stance their mother took when she stood, hands on her hips, after they had done something wrong.

"What a mess, boys! Let's try and get this poor man to a bed to rest. My data bank tells me that he's in some sort of shock." Roto reached out to help the apparently unconscious man. His antennae lights flashed in alarm. "Wha--I can't touch him!"

Axion and Zentin rushed forward to touch the form on the floor and gasped. They felt nothing but empty air. "Roto, what's happening?"

"I'm not sure, but I think that you may have beamed up Sir Henry's spirit."

"Spirit? Cool, you mean his ghost? Wow!" gasped Zentin.

"H-he's dead?" added Axion. "Did we kill him?"

"Of course not, Axion!" snapped Roto. He then searched his data. He was a robot who had been programmed with every possible fact from the beginning of time up until the present. Roto was daily updated from the central space station in the nearby galaxy of Starlet. He was the spaceship's source of ultimate knowledge. "My data bank tells me that Sir Henry last fought in the Battle of Bannockburn in Scotland on the 23rd June 1314 AD. Sir Henry was in the vanguard, or in modern language, the advance party of soldiers."

"Who was he fighting?" asked Zentin.

"Where's Bannockburn?" asked Axion.

"Shush! If you both keep quiet, I'll tell you. Don't make such a noise or we may lose Sir Henry's spirit--or if you prefer, ghost. Yes, Sir Henry must be a ghost. That explains the fading in and out, and why we can't feel him. His spirit is in shock. Wait a few moments until he regains alertness. Fan him with your cloak, Zentin. Yes, that's it. Look, Sir Henry's form is becoming clear again. Good, we haven't lost the spirit."

"You mean we actually beamed up a spirit from the past and not a live person?" asked Axion as he helped to fan the prostrate image on the floor. "Ace!"

"Roto, what happened next in the battle of Ban-whatever?" added Zentin.

"The correct name of the battle was Bannockburn, Zentin," replied Roto. "I will go back to the part where I was interrupted. My data bank has all the information in the history section, 14th Century England."

Axion prompted, "Sir Henry was in the English

vanguard."

"I said quiet, Axion!" snapped Roto. "The group came down across the meadow, their lines moved into a column to cross the burn."

"A burn?" asked Zentin.

"A burn is the Scottish word for a creek or stream. Now, stop interrupting!"

"Sorry, Roto. Carry on." Axion winked at Zentin.

The robot's voice echoed around the room as he continued the tale. "In the lead were Hereford and Gloucester. Fifty yards ahead of them, rode Sir Henry de Bohun, clad in full armour on a powerful horse with a spear in his hand. As he came through the trees on the north bank of the burn, he saw a lone rider inspecting the Scottish troops. This rider was half hidden in the woodland, atop a light saddle horse. He had an axe in his hand and a golden crown around his helmet."

"A crown? Which king, Roto?" whispered Axion as he anxiously fanned the vision lying on the floor.

"May I continue?" The twins nodded. "Good!" Roto's navigation lights were beginning to flash red in anger. "Sir Henry, here, recognized the King of Scots. He galloped towards the King. The King turned his horse and cantered towards him. As Sir Henry came near, Robert the Bruce swerved and rose up in his stirrups. He brought down his axe with such force on de Bohun's head that he cut through the helmet, breaking his axe handle in the process."

"Hey, Axion, that must be the scar on his spirit's head!" remarked Zentin.

"Erk, what a way to die!" Axion grimaced.

As Axion spoke, there was a soft groan from the knight. Roto's mechanism hissed as he moved closer and said, "Keep fanning him with your cloaks. Yes, his image is getting stronger. Good! We now have one complete ghost on board the spaceship. We must tell the Admiral."

"Dad? No! Please, Roto, don't tell him! Not for a while anyway. Please!" wined Axion. "Besides, Dad may not be able to see Sir Henry."

"Well, maybe he won't, maybe he will. My data bank agrees with your last comment, Axion. I note that Sir Henry's ghost is visible to all three of us. Usually, ghosts choose whom they want to show themselves to. Aha! Perhaps Sir Henry doesn't know he's dead!"

"Dead? I am not dead, Sir Roto!" grumbled Sir Henry who sat up. Then, with lots of *creaks, clunks* and *clangs,* he turned over onto his knees and bellowed, "Well, help me up, please!"

"I'm sorry, Sir Henry, but we can't. We can't feel or touch you!" giggled Axion.

"Nonsense, lad! Stand still and I will elevate myself by using ye as a support."

Axion stood still. Sir Henry stood up in front of him, also looking puzzled.

"Strange! I cannot feel thy hand or thy shoulder. *Ugh!* My hand can go straight through thy body!" Sir Henry gasped. "Are ye ghosts? Is this so-called place that ye call SS Ventura, a type of Heaven?"

Roto's staccato voice echoed around the transporter room. "No, Sir Henry, we are real. *You* are the ghost! King Robert the Bruce killed you when you charged at him at the Battle of Bannockburn. Try to remember. He hit you on the head with his axe."

"Oooooh, my head! Bruce killed me? I'm dead? Oh, no! I am dead!" Sir Henry walked around in a circle. He touched his head. Finally, he stopped, took his sword from its sheath, then knelt down onto one knee, laying the sword on the floor in front of Roto. "Ye speak with strange accents, similar to the Scots. I am, therefore, thy humble prisoner!"

Chapter 2
Ghost Tricks

Axion and Zentin stood and looked at the kneeling knight. It was the staccato-computerized voice of Roto that broke the silence. "One cannot make a ghost a prisoner. We also have not been at war with England, Scotland or against your people for centuries! Therefore, Sir Henry, we ask you to rise and pick up your sword. You are our honoured guest."

"I thank ye. What a strange place I find myself in." Sir Henry stood up and looked around the transporter room of the huge spaceship. "I like the beautiful lifelike paintings of stars and the night sky on the wall." He pointed to the windows, which revealed the Starlet galaxy's myriad of stars and planets beaming out against the ink-black void of space.

"Paintings?" Zentin giggled. "Sir Henry, those are windows."

A deep frown appeared on Sir Henry's bald head. "Windows? But they are huge! How can thee make such large windows?" He walked over to the nearest window and peered out. "Where is the ground?"

"We're flying around in space, Sir Henry," replied Axion.

"Nonsense! Only ghosts and witches can fly. I--err--I am flying? I am really a ghost? And ye are ghosts, too?"

"No, we're not ghosts, Sir Henry. Only *you* are," laughed Zentin.

"How old are ye?" ask Sir Henry.

"We are 8 years old," responded Zentin.

"But ye are so tall for that age. Are ye giants?"

Zentin laughed. "No! We are a normal height for our age. Dad says that centuries ago, people were shorter."

"I am--was a tall man in England," remarked Sir Henry. "How tall is thy father?"

"Dad's 7 feet 4 inches tall, I think," replied Axion.

Giants!

"Sir Henry," Axion said, "you can imagine that we are in a magic place that can fly around in the air. Does that help?"

"So, now ye are saying that ye are wizards! Aye, what

a strange place this is and what strange folk ye are! So, if ye are wizards and I am a ghost, then I can walk through the wall of this weird place!" With that last remark, Sir Henry *clanked* and *squeaked* across the room straight towards the outside shell of the spaceship.

"No! Don't! You'll die! Err, I mean, there's no air out there. Sir Henry?" gasped Zentin as the knight disappeared straight outside through the wall.

Oh my, I can walk through walls! Have these wizards caste a spell on me, or am I indeed a ghost?

A few seconds later, the smiling face of Sir Henry was peering inside at the speechless twins.

"Amazing! I must add this into my data base," remarked Roto.

Sir Henry walked back through the spaceship's outer casing and stood inside and, with a big grin, said, "Thy faces have turned pale, master wizards! That was fun. I think I will enjoy being a ghost. That is *if* I am a ghost." He pointed to the wall. "Now ye must do the same!"

Axion mumbled, "But we can't, Sir Henry. Not without putting on our space suits and going out through the exit chamber."

"Space suit? Pray, lad, what are ye talking about?"

"Well, Sir Henry, we need the suit so we can breathe air and so we won't be killed by the vacuum of space," replied Zentin.

"Vacuum?"

"It's a place or room without air--um--Sir Henry, I don't know how to explain it," responded Zentin.

Sir Henry looked at the wall, then promptly turned around and walked through it and outside. This time he strolled around from window to window, waving at the boys inside. At last, he walked in through the closed window, then stood with arms folded across his chest and grinned.

Axion and Zentin laughed.

"That was neat, Sir Henry! Wish we could do that. But as we've already told you, we can't without space suits," said Zentin.

Sir Henry smiled, saying, "Hmmm, I have to take thy word. But I still think that this is a magic place and ye are young wizards!"

A buzzing noise came from Axion's belt buckle. Axion touched the buckle with his forefinger. Sir Henry gasped as a woman's voice was heard. His eyes bulged, as he peered at Axion's belt.

"Axion? Zentin? It's time you two were in bed! I'll come to your bedroom in five minutes."

"Okay, Mum. We're just getting ready for bed now," responded Axion, talking to the buckle.

"Aye, 'tis indeed magic. Ye made the belt talk!" gasped the appreciative knight.

"It was our Mum speaking. I--hum--oh, never mind that now, Sir Henry. Quick! We have to hurry to our room before our mother gets there. Follow us!" said Zentin.

The Knight followed the twins through into the passageway. Roto followed with a quiet hiss. He muttered, "Oh, my! I think we are going to get into trouble!"

They finally stopped at a sliding door. Zentin placed his hand on a panel on the wall. The door slid silently open as his handprint was recognized.

"Come inside, Sir Henry. This will take us to our room above," whispered Axion.

"How did that door open?" asked Sir Henry.

"It's magic!" grinned Zentin. "Hold on, Sir Henry, we're going for a short ride."

Sir Henry gasped as the small room moved and seemed to go sideways for a few moments before moving up and stopping. "Aye, 'tis a magic place!" The door slid open again and they moved out into a large comfortable room with two beds in the corner.

"Welcome to our sleeping quarters, Sir Henry," said Axion.

Zentin turned to Roto and quickly said, "Roto, you'd better go back to the deck before dad wonders where you've disappeared to. I don't want to see you get into trouble."

"I will do as you command, Master Zentin," replied Roto, and added, "Take care, Axion. And Sir Henry, please do not make yourself visible to anyone else until we tell you it's safe to do so. Good night." Roto moved quietly out of the room into the transport capsule.

Sir Henry sighed. "What a gallant knight Sir Roto is, young masters. If I am indeed a ghost, methinks that I shall not be able to disappear and reappear as he wishes. I am so confused."

"Perhaps if you think about the possibility, it may happen, Sir Henry," replied Zentin. "Hey, try it now, before Mum comes."

Sir Henry frowned as if in deep concentration. His image started to disappear!

"Wow!" gasped Axion. "You've done it, Sir Henry. Hey, where are you?"

Clank. Squeak. Clink.

"Hum, I think you'd better remember to make those sounds of your armour disappear, too," Axion laughed.

There was silence. The creaking armour noises stopped. "Cool! Well done, Sir Henry."

"Who is Sir Henry?" asked Lythia, their mother. She had entered the room just after the knight had vanished from sight.

Axion and Zentin spun around in fright. "Mum, you

sneaked in!"

"What have you both been up to?"

"Nothing, Mum," was the chorused reply.

"We were only pretending that we were knights in shining armour back in the 14th century," added Axion.

"What imaginations you both have! All right, it's time you got some sleep. We'll be stopping at Xet tomorrow for supplies of fresh water and food."

"Hooray!" exclaimed Axion. "I'm getting sick of the packaged muck!"

"Axion, you must stop criticizing the chef's menus. He does his best when we are travelling. I'll be glad when school starts again after the vacation break. It will keep you two out of trouble." She smiled, then added, "Good night, boys. I'll see you both at breakfast time."

The now invisible Sir Henry watched, spellbound, as the tall 6 foot 4 inch Lythia moved gracefully across the twin's room. She entered the transport capsule and waved as the door closed. *She is so tall. These people are like giants.*

Axion and Zentin waited for a few moments before daring to call out to Sir Henry.

"Sir Henry? Are you still here?" asked Zentin.

The twins jumped in surprise as his form abruptly appeared in front of them. "I did not leave, Master Zentin. I simply disappeared from thy sight, and more importantly, from thy mother's sight. She is a handsome woman."

"She's okay, I guess! I don't know about the 'handsome' bit though. Dad calls her sexy." Axion chuckled.

"Masters, ye are very forthright in your comments, I must declare!" gasped Sir Henry. "Sexy indeed! That is not a proper way to describe one's mother. 'Beautiful' is a more appropriate word. Now, ye should get some sleep, as thy mother requested."

"Not yet, Sir Henry, I'm too excited to sleep. Hey, could you tell us about the battle of Bannockburn?" asked Axion, sitting up in his bed, arms wrapped around his knees. "Please, please!"

"Right, Master Axion, Master Zentin. I am thy humble servant. Thy wish is my command. I shall tell ye about the Battle of Bannockburn. Well, as much of it as I can remember, before that rogue, Bruce, hit me! *Humph!*"

The twins sat in awe as the ghost of the 14th century English knight started his tale.

Chapter 3
The Ghost's Tale

Sir Henry looked at the eager faces. They were identical, with the exception of one small birthmark on Axion's left cheek. He found it hard to believe that they were not young wizards in disguise. Even the knight who called himself Roto was, indeed, different from any other knight he'd seen in his travels. In fact, Axion and Zentin looked exactly like two innocent young *Cnigt's* or boys. *They are like me as a young page in training to be a knight to the King of England.* Sir Henry's heart softened. He felt a special bond growing between his spirit and those of the twins. Making himself comfortable, he sat on the padded bench near the boy's bunks, cleared his throat and started his tale.

"I believe ye already know the story of the Battle of Bannockburn, so I shall tell ye a tale about a young boy of eight, called Henry de Bohun."

"That's you?" asked Axion.

"Aye, lad, ye are correct. I was only eight when my father, an English nobleman, sent me to the neighbouring castle to be trained as a page."

"What's a page?" asked Zentin.

"A page is the son of a knight, or a member of the aristocracy. As such, I spent most days strengthening my body, wrestling and riding horses. I also learned how to fight with spear and sword."

"Wow!" Zentin moved forward, his eyes wide.

"I practiced against a wooden dummy called a *quintain*. This, before ye ask, is a heavy sack or dummy in the form of a person. It was hung on a wooden pole along with a shield. My task was to hit the shield in its centre, then move away quickly before it spun around and hit me. I was also taught to read and write."

"There was school back in your days, too, huh, Sir Henry?" sighed Axion.

Sir Henry laughed. He really was beginning to enjoy himself. It was also nice to have such an attentive audience. "The lady of the house taught me, as a page, to sing and dance and how to behave in the king's court.

When I was sixteen, I became a squire in service to a knight. My duties included dressing the knight in the morning, serving all of the knight's meals, caring for his horse and cleaning his armour and weapons."

"You were a servant?" Axion asked.

"Nay, lad, not a servant--I was a squire in service--or training if ye like. I even followed my knight to tournaments and assisted him on the battlefield. At this time, I learned to handle a sword and lance while wearing forty pounds of armour and riding a horse."

"Hey, that's some trick, Sir Henry. I didn't realize that armour weighed that much!" exclaimed Zentin.

"On my twentieth birthday, I became a knight."

"How? Did you have to sit an exam or something?" interrupted Axion. He moved closer to the end of his bunk, rolled onto his tummy and rested his head on his arms.

"*Ahem!* I simply had to prove myself worthy of the title. The evening before the dubbing ceremony, I dressed in a white tunic and red robes."

"Dubbing?" asked Zentin.

"Dubbing is a name for giving authority to someone," replied Sir Henry.

"Just like dad being made an Admiral," remarked Zentin.

"Aye, Master Zentin."

"What happened next?" Axion asked.

"I fasted and prayed all night for the purification of my soul. The chaplains blessed my sword and laid it on the church's altar. Just before dawn, I took a bath to show I was pure and then dressed in my best clothes."

"A religious service?" asked Axion.

"That is a good description, Master Axion," replied Sir Henry.

"What happened next," Zentin asked.

"At dawn, the priest came and heard my confession. I then ate breakfast, after which I was ready for the outdoor ceremony. The ceremony was done in front of my family, friends, and nobility. I knelt in front of the lord, who tapped me lightly on each shoulder with his sword."

"I've seen a picture of a nobleman using his sword like that," remarked Axion. "It was a history book."

Sir Henry smiled, and continued. "I was named Sir Henry de Bohun, a knight in service to the King of England."

"Did you fight in any wars?" asked Axion.

"Aye, Master Axion. I fought in some battles and tournaments."

"A tournament is where the knights competed against each other, isn't it, Sir Henry? Didn't you charge at each other with a spear and try and knock each other off your horses? You fought each other with swords and thumped each other on the head with a big spiked stick!"

Sir Henry laughed, and in his deep voice said, "Well, that would be the most accurate description that I have heard about a tournament in years. Ho! Ho! Ooh, now my head aches again."

"Can we get you some headache pills?" asked Zentin anxiously.

"Nay, ye should not worry. As we have found out, as a ghost, I shall not be in need of such magic potion, lad. But I thank ye for the kind thought." Sir Henry noted that the two boys were beginning to look sleepy. "I think ye should now both try and sleep. I will stand guard 'till morning. Perhaps I shall not need to sleep again. Ghosts are in the land of everlasting sleep, are they not?"

"Dunno, Sir Henry. Perhaps Roto could answer that one. You're right. It's late." Axion yawned and added, "Don't go away, will you?"

"Nay, Master Axion, Master Zentin, a knight is always true to his word. As promised, I shall stand guard whilst ye sleep. Good night, Masters."

"G'night."

"Night, Sir Henry."

As the spaceship sped on through the ink black darkness of space outside, the knight sat in the chair, keeping watch over the twins. His thoughts went back to his last memory of life when he had charged at King Robert the Bruce of Scotland.

Chapter 4
Secrets!

Hours had passed, yet the sky was still pitch black outside the boys' bedroom window. Sir Henry walked over to the window and marvelled at the stars. He gasped as he saw a big object appearing. It looked like an enormous moon. Hearing movement from the boy's bunks, he turned to see Axion stretching and getting up.

"Good morning, Master Axion."

"Argh! Sir Henry! Heck, you gave me a fright. You're invisible."

Sir Henry made himself visible again. He watched as Zentin opened his eyes and sat up.

"You're still here? Ace! Hey, I dreamed about you last

night, Sir Henry. You were riding your horse, and you were in full armour. Your horse had armour on, too. You were charging at an alien's space ship that was attacking us. Dreams are often weird, aren't they?" remarked Axion.

Zentin looked at his brother and laughed. "Trust you to dream something like that! Come on, it's shower time. Bet I'm first to the dining room for breakfast!"

Sir Henry was intrigued. The boys went into a tiny adjacent room. His spirit followed them. He watched as they touched a knob and a spray of soft soapy water poured over their naked bodies. He shook his head in amazement as they pressed another button and the water flow stopped. They each stood on a mat, and warm air blew out over them, drying them. They quickly dressed and raced to the transport capsule door. Sir Henry thought, *I must keep them in view.* In reply to this thought, he was instantly beside them as the capsule moved silently up and round, then stopped.

"Don't forget, Sir Henry, you must remain invisible and silent to anyone else except the two of us and Roto. You're our secret, okay?"

Sir Henry's forehead wrinkled into a puzzled expression as he spoke. "Okay? What strange language ye speak, lad. What does 'okay' mean?"

"Ah! Sir Henry, don't keep appearing like that! If any

anyone sees you, they'll freak out!" gasped Axion.

Zentin smiled. "Axion's right. Please stay invisible and only let us hear what you want to say. Now, to answer your question, 'okay' means 'all right'."

"Ah! Thank thee for the explanation, young Zentin. Hmmm, I should say 'okay'?" he replied, his laugh booming inside their heads. "I shall do as thee command, Masters," replied Sir Henry and instantly became invisible as the capsule door opened. The twins walked out into a warm room filled with delicious aromas.

Sir Henry delighted in the smells permeating from the kitchen. He remained invisible and happily cruised around, peering into the pots and looking at the plates. *Strange, how despite enjoying the smell of the food, I'm not hungry. Of course, ghosts don't eat! What interesting looking food.* Sir Henry followed the cook as he carried the food to the dining area.

Axion and Zentin sat at the table with their mother. Sir Henry looked at Admiral Trebor. *Yes, the boys were correct. He is over 7 feet tall--almost a giant! All these people in the future are so tall and well-built.* Sir Henry was now beginning to enjoy the fact that he could listen to conversations without being seen. *This is one of the best features of being a ghost.* The Admiral started to talk as Sir Henry moved invisibly around the room.

"What have you two been doing? I haven't seen much of you at all lately."

Axion and Zentin started to talk almost together, as if reading each other's thoughts. They helped each other by finishing each other's sentences. Sir Henry had seen twins back in the 14th century with this ability. He realized that the twins had the same sandy coloured hair as their father, but their mother's green eyes. *Do they have Celtic blood in their veins? A lot of the Scottish lads I met had light or ginger hair.*

"Well, Father, we've been reading--" started Axion.

"About life back in the olden days on earth--" continued Zentin.

"We found stuff on knights back in the 14th century--" added Axion.

"As boys, they were sent away from their homes to another castle to learn--" prompted Zentin.

"How to fight and sing and dance like a knight," finished Zentin.

"I wish you two would finish one of your own sentences for a change," laughed the Admiral. "I never know which one of you to look at when you both start talking like that. What prompted you to research ancient history? I thought you hated learning history?"

"Well, we um--err--found a book called *Camelot*," started Axion.

"The knights wore really neat stuff, Dad," concluded Zentin. "We thought we'd give history a bit of a go. That's all."

Sir Henry smiled. The boys had obviously been impressed by his tale the previous evening. He really wanted to show himself to the Admiral and tell him that he was the cause of this excitement. But his code of honour and chivalry as a knight had to be kept. He must keep his promise to remain invisible and silent to everyone except Axion and Zentin and, of course Roto, the modern knight in strange-looking armour.

Sir Henry wanted to ask the boys what the strange, brown flakes were in their bowls. They added what looked like milk out a box. *Forsooth, perhaps they are wizards! Milk comes from cows in the field, not magically from a little box on the table!* But Sir Henry stayed invisible to keep the children's secret. Instead, he drifted around the table to look at the other plates.

"*Brr,* there's a draft wafting around this room this morning," exclaimed the Admiral. He pressed a bracelet on his left wrist and spoke into it. Sir Henry felt like a curious little boy again. He rushed over to see what the Admiral was using on his wrist. "*Brr,* there it is again. Sparks? This is the Admiral. Could you check the air temperature in the dining room? There's a cold draft in here this morning. Yes, I agree it's strange."

Sir Henry forgot to remain invisible.

Axion gasped, his eyes opening wide. Zentin, dropped his spoon spilling some of the cereal on the table. "Oops! Sorry about that. Must have been daydreaming."

"Nonsense, Zentin! Daydreaming? Never! Now, if you were Axion, I'd not be surprised," smiled his mother.

Axion gave a cheeky grin, "Perhaps the cold air is a ghost drifting around. You know, one that's *invisible*-- Ouch!" Zentin had kicked him under the table.

Axion's emphasis on the word *invisible* caught Sir Henry's previously wandering attention. He made himself invisible again. He wondered when these two fascinating boys would tell their parents about him. At first, it had been rather fun to be a secret, but now he wanted to talk to the adults as well as the children. There were so many questions that needed answers. He was beginning to believe that he was indeed now in a future time. *Perhaps some wizard hidden in the Scottish Army at Bannockburn has changed me into a spirit to play tricks with me. Aye, this so-called spaceship is a mysterious place. The people here speak to their wrists! The lad Axion has also spoken to his belt. All these things are indeed magic!*

As the family finished their meal, the admiral stood up, startling Sir Henry from his thoughts, making him forget to remain silent. His metal armour made its usual noises as he moved back out of the Admiral's way. *Squeak! Clink! Clonk!*

"What on earth?" Admiral Trebor spun around, then turned around facing his sons again and laughed. "Goodness, your talk of ghosts is making me hear and see things that aren't there. Everyone knows there aren't such things as ghosts!" He glanced at his wrist again. "Well, I must get back to the flight deck. We will be approaching planet Xet in another two hours. I'll get Roto to check the beam transporter so we will be able to beam up our food supplies when we reach their atmosphere."

"May we go to the flight deck when we approach Xet, Dad?" asked Zentin.

"Of course, but I want you both to sit still and not touch anything! I know you like to fiddle with things, especially the transporter."

"But, Dad, we only touched the things that we knew about," started Axion, but stopped when Zentin nudged him.

"Ha! So, you have been down in the transporter room! That's an urgent reason for Roto to check the settings. I'll send Griff Sparks to help." He scowled. "Now, I want you both to promise **not** to touch the transporter again."

"Yes, sir!" they replied in unison.

With those final instructions, their father strode across the room to the sliding doors of the little moveable capsule. As he put his hand on the touch pad, he turned. The anger had disappeared from his face. "I'll see you both up on the flight deck in one and a half hours."

"Yes, Sir," they replied in unison, standing stiff at attention.

"Are you going to beam down to Xet, Mum?" asked Axion.

"No, but I'll join you in the transporter room to watch the supplies being beamed up. Now, promise me not to fiddle with the space transporter again. It not only makes your father angry, it's dangerous!"

"Yes, Mum!" they replied in chorus.

With that last remark, their mother rose, touched the hand pad and disappeared through the sliding doors.

"Surely magic moved those doors!" Sir Henry's voice startled the boys. "I noted that neither of ye mentioned the word 'promise' to thy parents."

"Well, we can't promise not to touch the transporter again. One day you may want to return to 14th century England." Zentin grinned.

"I'd be alive?"

"No, 'fraid not. Roto's data base says that once you're dead, that's it!" replied Zentin.

Sir Henry sighed.

Axion grinned at him. "Gosh, you nearly blew it by starting to become visible behind Dad! And that was so funny when your armour clanked when Dad stood up to leave the table. The look on Dad's face was so puzzled when he saw a bit of your spirit. It looked just like a bit of smoke hanging there, then zap, gone! Now, that's what I call a magic trick, Sir Henry." Axion laughed. "It's fun having you as a secret, but I just wish that we could show you."

"No, Axion, we can't. Perhaps we can later. Father isn't happy about us being in the transporter room as it is. He'll hit the roof if he finds out that we played with the settings."

"Oh, he'll find out, Zentin. He always does!" added Axion.

Sir Henry followed them to the capsule's doors and entered through the sliding doors when they opened. They travelled back through the space ship towards the sleeping area.

The doors opened from the travel tube revealing the boy's bedroom again. Sir Henry's ghost-like form followed the boys. He watched, fascinated, as they used the different objects in the smaller adjacent room. The boys explained that this little room was the bath cubicle. Axion and Zentin roared with laughter as Sir Henry inspected the next cubicle and the seat with the hole in it.

"That's our toilet." Axion grinned.

"I realised that master Axion. But this is a wonderful design," exclaimed Sir Henry.

"What where your toilets like?" asked Zentin.

"Well, sires, we simply went into the bushes, or dug a hole. In the castles, there were holes in the walls where we could relieve ourselves into the moat outside. The new castles were installing *garderobes.*"

"Garderobes?"

"Ah yes, garderobes are like the first toilets, methinks. Each was recessed into the wall, in which there were stone ledges to carry the seats. The shafts led into a pit below. A stream of water would be diverted to flush it clean. So thy toilets are not fancy gadgets after all!" concluded Sir Henry triumphantly.

"Yuck! That wasn't very hygienic, Sir Henry!" snorted Axion, pulling a face.

"Axion, they didn't have sewerage or our type of plumbing in the 14th Century!" laughed Zentin.

Axion grunted.

"Masters, I wish ye to promise on the knight's oath, using my sword, that one day, ye will reveal me to thy parents. As a knight, or a ghost knight, I still wish to serve ye. I am sworn to chivalry to help defend ye all!"

Axion and Zentin looked at the proud ghost standing in front of them.

"But, Sir Henry, there's no need for chivalry. We aren't at war," Zentin remarked.

"Sir Henry, we'll promise that if we need you to help us, we will call on your devoted service."

"Thank ye, young Masters!"

"Now, Sir Henry, you can come with us to the flight deck." Zentin frowned and added, "But please, please, please don't make any noises or show yourself to anyone."

"Yeah, Sir Henry, you can see how this space ship moves and can visit other planets. Want to come to the flight deck with us?" asked Axion.

"Aye, I do, young man. But remember, I can go anywhere now, at anytime if I need to--except go back to my past life. All right, lead the way, Sires. I promise I shall be near with my sword ready at all times!"

Chapter 5
Space 3000 AD

The twins, Axion and Zentin, went to the flight deck of the SS Ventura, via the transport tube. Sir Henry, true to his word, remained both invisible and silent to everyone in the room. He peered at the flight deck. It had large clear windows on one side and strange-looking seats with woven straps on them. A large structure spread across the base of the windows. *Bright candles? Nay, they are not candles! What made such strong steady glows of light with so many different colours?* The genial ghost's thoughts transferred to Axion, who was the more receptive of the twins.

Axion, smiled and said, "I love seeing all the lights flashing on the control panel, Captain Dreamer. One day

I want to control a space ship like you do and move this joystick." Axion deliberately pointed to the control lever as he continued. "I could turn the ship to the left or to the right or go up or go down."

"What made you say that, Axion?" Captain Dreamer frowned. "You've seen this panel hundreds of times." The captain laughed, and Zentin joined in the laughter, as did their father, Admiral Trebor.

Axion's face flushed.

Sir Henry's spirit felt strongly for Axion. *At his age, I was easily embarrassed.* He transferred his thoughts to the still red-faced boy, thanking him for explaining what the strange things in front of him were used for. Outside the window, planet Xet started to grow bigger and bigger. The spaceship flew over the ground below. *This is like flying as a bird!* It was such a different scene from planet Earth. Everything glowed with a strange reddish colour. *These colours are like the setting sun's glow over my father's castle and land in England.*

"Fasten your seat belts, everyone!" commanded Captain Dreamer.

Sir Henry suddenly realized what the woven straps were for on each seat. For five minutes, the captain moved the so-called joystick around in deft hands. Finally, there was a mild shudder and the SS Ventura stopped moving, hovering above this strange land. "Wait until I get the 'all clear' for the atmosphere reading. Oxygen levels excellent--same as Earth." Captain Dreamer turned to his commander, Admiral Trebor. "Sir, our supplies are ready to be beamed up from Xet."

"Thanks, Captain. Stand by here. I'm going to the transporter room. If you need me, call me on my transceiver."

"Yes, sir!" replied Captain Dreamer.

Admiral Trebor turned to Axion and Zentin. "Now boys, it's time for us to go to the transporter room."

Sir Henry didn't follow them into the transport tube. He knew where this so-called transporter room was. After all, it was the room where he had first arrived into this peculiar world! He zapped himself through the structure of the ship. This newfound experience of being able to go through walls was fun! He arrived there before them. To his surprise, he found Roto, his companion space knight hovering near the platform. Roto's staccato voice echoed around the otherwise empty room.

"Hello, Sir Henry. I'm glad you got here first. I see you are beginning to find your own way around this spaceship. That's good."

"But how--err, I'm invisible, sir! How can ye see my spirit?"

"Aha! That's my secret. No, I shouldn't tease you, Sir Henry. As a computer, I have electronic sensors that can pick up any change in vibrations, or occurrences in the atmosphere. My visual database is, in this regard, better than human eyes, because I can see the invisible! But don't tell the boys that. It's my secret from them, for now anyway. I hope--" Roto stopped in mid-sentence. The Admiral and his sons came into the transporter room. "Everything is ready for the transportation, Admiral."

Sir Henry watched the platform. The shield on the platform filled with swirling cloud. The mist suddenly cleared, revealing boxes containing vegetables and other strange objects. *So, this must be the ship supplies, which the Admiral had mentioned.*

"Scientific miracle, huh?" remarked Zentin.

Axion thought, *it's a way of moving things, similar to how Sir Henry can now travel as a ghost.*

Sir Henry's responded via thought transfer.

Thank you, Master Axion. It seems that we can transfer thoughts to each other! Magic, indeed!

A screen appeared out from the top of the transporter table, startling Sir Henry so much that his form appeared briefly behind the Admiral.

"Brr," the Admiral said. "There's that darn cold draft again. Did you feel it, Sparks?"

"Yes, sir, I did. Strange, but it didn't show up on my meter analysis."

Roto checked on the transporter viewing screen, which showed where and what the transporter was doing. It was electronically locked onto anything that entered the transporter system.

"Maybe it's a ghost!" giggled Axion. "Ouch!" Zentin had elbowed him.

"That's the second time you've mentioned ghosts this morning, young man," grumbled his father. "You've been reading too many medieval stories."

Axion blushed again, and watched as the boxes containing fresh food and water were packed into the transport tube. Sparks programmed the transport tube to take the supplies up to the kitchen. Sir Henry watched, as Admiral Trebor conversed with Captain Dreamer through his wrist gadget. He had found out earlier that it was a transmitter. *More magic! I transmitted messages via carrier pigeon over long distances. Over short distances, a message on parchment was wrapped around an arrow and fired from a bow, from one archer to another. Pigeons were quick, but this transmitter of the future is real magic.*

The admiral and Engineer Sparks returned to the flight deck, advising the boys and Roto to prepare for the spaceship's departure from Xet's atmosphere.

"Xet looks just like Earth, except for the strange golden glow," remarked Sir Henry once he was alone with the boys and Roto.

Roto's metallic sounding voice replied, "Planet Xet has the same atmosphere as Earth, and the people who you saw on the computer screen on the transporter panel here are astronauts from Earth. We have people operating stations on other similar planets. They are creating new settlements for humans. Earth is now becoming too crowded. These settlements, once self-sufficient, can also help replenish supplies for space ships and space stations around the universe."

"Come on, Sir Henry, we're going back to the flight deck. It's fun to watch as we zoom off back into space. Our next stop is our own Space Station Explorer, which rotates around the moon, near Earth. I'm sure you'd like to see what earth looks like from Space!" exclaimed Zentin.

"The Earth will look like a plate, because it is flat," replied Sir Henry.

"Flat?" Axion and Zentin dissolved into laughter. "You say such funny things sometimes, Sir Henry! The world is round like a ball. You'll see for yourself when we get there."

This time, Sir Henry was determined to beat the boys' back to the flight deck. He was full of curiosity.

"Thank thee for an interesting experience, Sir Roto! Now I must leave and get to the flight deck before them." He bowed to Roto. "I thank thee, good Sir Roto." With those words, Sir Henry disappeared from Roto's sight.

Sir Henry settled himself at the flight deck, watching the flashing lights on the table and the stars flashing past the front window. Later, the whole family- Axion, Zentin, Admiral Trebor and his wife Lythia - were all together and peering out through the front. He deliberately kept himself invisible. After all, he had sworn an oath of secrecy to his new young masters. The SS Venture hurled faster than the speed of light through space, towards the far end of the Galaxy of Starlet, the new name for the Earth's galaxy. The enormous space station Explorer rotated around a small white planet. *It looks just like the moon in the sky.*

"It's good to see the moon again, huh Dad?" remarked Zentin.

So this is the moon! How strange that it is now so big. Ah! And what was that big ball over yonder?

"Much nicer to see Earth again I reckon," smiled Axion. "Hey, it's only a few months until we can spend our holidays there."

I wonder if the moon has green cheese, like nanny had told me. Is there really a 'man in the moon'? Maybe that the 'green cheese' and 'man in the moon' are only fables! Sir Henry's thoughts were interrupted as Captain

Dreamer's voice came from a little box on the nearby wall. "Everyone, please take your docking positions! We will dock with the Space Station Explorer in exactly five minutes."

Axion, Zentin and Lythia went to some chairs in the room they called the living room. The chairs had straps attached, just like the chairs in the flight deck. They strapped themselves in and sat patiently. Sir Henry spirited himself to the flight deck to see firsthand what was happening. His eyes widened at the sight in front of the spaceship. *The Space Station Explorer is huge. It is more than twice the size of my father's castle. What a wonderful sight!* He leaned over Captain Zac Dreamer's shoulder.

"*Brr,* there's that confounded draft again, Admiral. My shoulder's half frozen with cold!"

Sir Henry removed his invisible hand off the captain's shoulder.

"I'll get the engineers to go over the ship from top to bottom before we set out again," said Dreamer.

Two doors appeared in the side of the space structure outside the window ahead. The spaceship was deftly manoeuvred through these doors and onto a landing platform. The ship shuddered slightly, and then there was silence.

"Docking is complete. Seat belts off." Admiral Trebor

spoke into a little button on the end of a curved wire near his mouth.

Sir Henry later learned that this was a mini microphone. Axion and Zentin rushed off the space ship and ran off to meet and play with several other children. Sir Henry quickly spirited himself off the spaceship and started to explore the space station alone. It was several hours later before Sir Henry had the chance to find some solutions to the dozens of questions that he had mentally compiled. At last, the boys had finished their evening meal and had gone to their sleeping quarters. They were on their own.

Clink! Clank! Clunk! "Well, young masters, it has, indeed, been a most interesting and educational day!" he exclaimed, appearing at the end of Axion's bed.

"Sir Henry, I wish you wouldn't suddenly appear without warning," laughed Zentin. "Why don't you take your armour off while inside the space station? You'd be much more comfortable."

"Aye, that I would, Master Zentin," replied Sir Henry. He took off his helmet, untied the leather straps on his breastplate, arms defenses, gauntlets, and leggings. The twins were fascinated and asked what each piece was called.

"Hey, Sir Henry, that material looks like chains welded together," exclaimed Axion.

"This is my mid-sleeve chain-mail hauberk. It is hard for arrows to penetrate the chain mail. The main problem is that this armour is so heavy!" Sir Henry finally stood before them wearing a pair of long woollen pants and a linen shirt. "Ah, ye were quite right. I am comfortable now, masters. I thank thee." He bowed to each of them. "May I show myself to the other children tomorrow?"

"Let's keep you our secret, a little longer, Sir Henry. We need to find a good moment to explain your presence to our father first," replied Zentin.

"We'll have to tell him sooner or later, as Dad will find out somehow. He always does," added Axion sleepily.

Sir Henry nodded in agreement. He watched the twins drift off into a deep sleep. Sir Henry kept vigil, his sword nearby should his young masters' need protection.

Chapter 6
The 14th Century

When Axion and Zentin woke the next morning, they were shocked to find that Sir Henry had disappeared. They rushed around the enormous space station, politely knocking on the metallic doors of other families' living quarters. Each time, they invited themselves in, using the excuse, "We just wanted to say hello, after such a long trip."

They finally had to stop, when their mother called them for lunch. Everyone gathered in the main dining room. Sir Henry had noted during his own exploration of the space station earlier, that the dining room was as big as any mediaeval one, except that the ceilings were much lower.

"Where is he?" whispered Zentin crossly. "At least he could have told us he wanted to leave!"

"Yes, he should have said good-bye," Axion sighed. "He must have had good reasons to disappear into thin air again."

"What are you two whispering about?" asked Lythia, peering across the table at her sons.

"Nothing, Mum. Nothing at all." Zentin gasped as he felt an ice-cold hand gently touch his left shoulder. "*Brr, bit of a cold draft in here, huh!*"

"Yes, that's strange. The engineer couldn't find anything wrong with the air-conditioning."

"They won't--" said Axion.

"What?"

"Shush, Axion, not now!" whispered Zentin crossly.

"Not now what? What are you two hiding?" demanded their father. "First you play around with the transporter on the space ship, and since then you've both been chattering incessantly, stating obvious facts for no reason--"

"Honestly Dad, it's nothing. It's just a pretend game we've been playing, that's all," replied Axion, quietly, frantically using his more creative mind to find a good answer. It was too early to tell their father about Sir Henry. "We've been pretending that we are knights of the 14th Century."

Their father started to laugh. "At least knights are honourable. I admire your choice of hero. It's time you left here to play or visit your friends. I'll be glad when schooling starts again next week." The twins scampered toward the door of the dining room, while their father was still in good humour. "Knights, indeed," he laughed, as they left.

Back in their sleeping quarters, with the door firmly shut, Axion and Zentin quietly called out to Sir Henry.

"Yes, masters?"

Zentin spoke first, his fists clenched in anger as he spat out his words. "You nearly messed up everything, Sir Henry. Why did you grab my shoulder like that?"

"Sire, I merely touched thy shoulder to let ye know I was back," he replied. "If ye wish to become a knight, ye must learn to control that quick temper, Master Zentin."

"Sir Henry is right, Zentin. You nearly told him our secret! It's too early to tell father--returned? Where from? Where have you been, Sir Henry?"

"I have been back to England, back to the 14th Century. Sir Roto helped me. We did it secretly. The bigger transporter in this Magic Space Castle worked beautifully. Sir Roto told me that he has all the details in that magic database of his. I asked him to help me. I wanted to see for myself, what exactly happened after the Battle of Bannockburn." Sir Henry knelt down on one knee, head bowed, "Please forgive me, sires."

"Wow, you actually went back to where we found you?" said an excited Axion.

"Hey, that's neat! What was it like? Did you find your friends? What happened?" added Zentin.

Sir Henry smiled, stood up and said, "One question at a time, sires. It was a sad experience. Many fellow knights died in that bloody battle. I can now see the point in thy argument, Master Zentin, that wars are fruitless!"

The twins felt saddened. Hundreds of years earlier, a nuclear war had nearly destroyed Planet Earth. Wise leaders had kept world peace. All nations signed a Universal Peace Program. Because of universal cooperation, the planet Earth had been a peaceful planet for over 500 years. The Space Station Explorer was one of several stations positioned in space, and there were now other habitable planets, like Xet, supporting human life on them.

Sir Henry looked at the sad faces, then smiled. "Would ye like to travel back to the 14th Century with me?"

"Of course!"

"Wow! That's fantastic! Can we go now?"

In their excitement, the twins spoke in unison.

"Aye, ye can go but ye cannot go just now. Ye will

have to wait until everyone sleeps tonight, masters. Sir Roto told me that a four-hour period would be enough time for our trip. He also told me that it would have to be in secret, like my trip today. This is another secret that we share, is it not?"

The twins could hardly contain their excitement. They wanted to tell their friends what was going to happen. It took a lot of willpower to keep their big secret. At the evening meal their mother remarked, "Slow down or you will get indigestion."

At last, it was time to retire to their sleeping quarters on the Space station. Each family or group had a specified private area where each could spend time together. However, it was still different from home, back on Earth. They pretended sleepiness when their parents came to say good night to them.

"Gosh, I'm tired, Mum," said Zentin.

"Yeah, we have been rushing around since we returned," added Axion.

The excitement of the time travel kept them awake. They waited until it was quiet. Finally, everyone, except the control deck crew, was asleep. Axion and Zentin opened the sliding door to their travel tube, using their palm prints for identification.

"Sir Henry, come on, or you will be late," whispered Zentin.

"Ye do not have to concern thyself about me. Remember, I can travel through walls without using thy travel box," Sir Henry replied, then promptly disappeared from their sight.

"Darn it, Axion, I bet he's in the transporter room already," laughed Zentin as he pressed the button labelled 'transporter room'. Roto and Sir Henry were waiting for their arrival, both standing next to the transporter platform.

Axion and Zentin were so excited that they started talking at the same time.

"Are we really going back in time?"

"Will it be dangerous?"

"How long will it take?"

"I bet Dad finds out. He always does," added Axion looking pensive.

Roto held up his mechanical arm and interrupted their chatter. "Axion, Zentin, hush, or your father will certainly find out. I've advised the control room crew that I'm doing some maintenance on the transporter, so they will not panic when they see the light come on in the flight deck. Now, as far as it being dangerous--well, no it won't be. I'm only sending your spirits down, not your physical bodies. I've worked out, from Sir Henry's composition or spiritual makeup, that you humans also have what some religions call a soul, or spirit. Others call it your personality. It's inside your physical bodies whilst alive, but becomes your spirit after you die. Well, I think that's what happens. My data bank has much conflicting information about this subject. Maybe you can discuss this with your parents sometime, or with your teachers at school."

"I hate school," exclaimed Zentin.

"Don't say such rubbish, Zentin! You love reading and writing and art and learning history. That's schoolwork," Roto responded in his almost comical staccato computer voice. "Come, don't dawdle, or you won't have time to spend at the other end. I'm gearing the transporter to bring all of your spirits back after four hours. I'll contact you on your transmitters when the time is up."

Axion and Zentin stood together on the platform with Sir Henry, who had kept his spirit visible.

"Is everyone ready? Remember that it's only your spirits going back to England in the 14th Century. No one will be able to see, feel or hear you. Above all, keep those belts on so I can track you on the transporter."

"Yes, Roto," said Axion.

"Okay, Roto," added Zentin.

"Thank ye, Sir Roto, for letting me show the boys my home!" smiled Sir Henry.

Roto pulled the switch and the dome moved over the three forms as the mist gathered around them.

"I don't feel anything! I thought it would be different from a normal transportation!" grumbled Zentin.

"Shush, Zentin. Listen!" snapped Axion. Suddenly the roar of a distant wind came closer and the mist began to swirl about, forming a small tornado-like cone around them. The suction formed by the mini tornado seemed to lift them out of their bodies. "Yeeeeoweeee! It's like flying through space without a space ship," called out Axion. The spinning cloud disappeared as suddenly as it came, leaving Axion, Zentin and Sir Henry standing in the middle of a field of dewy grass.

"Moooo!"

"Argh!" Axion attempted to step out of the path of the large cow, which was wandering around chewing its cud. However, before he moved, the cow calmly walked right through him! "Zentin, did you see that? We're just like Sir Henry. We're invisible to everything else except each other! We are just like ghosts!"

"We can't be ghosts, dummy!" replied Zentin, "'Cuz we haven't been born yet! Neither have Mum or Dad, or most of our ancestors. Hey, Sir Henry, this must be after the Battle of Bannockburn when you were killed 'coz the other cow just walked through you, too!" He stopped and looked at the still silent Sir Henry de Bohun. "What's wrong, Sir Henry?"

"That's my father's castle."

The twins looked to where he was pointing. Out of the evening mist rose a beautiful castle, complete with moat, drawbridge and towers.

Axion's eyes bulged with excitement. "It's just like the one in the *Camelot* book."

"There is no such place, sire," replied Sir Henry, and rushed off leaving a trail like a small jet stream behind him. "Hurry up, or ye shall not have enough time to see inside."

The twins' spirits followed in his wake, enjoying the freedom of not being inside their human forms. "Heee haaaa!" squealed Zentin.

"Sir Henry?" gasped Axion, looking up at the towering walls.

"Yes, sire?"

"How long did it take to build this?"

"I believe it took about 12 years to build. Some castles like this one took over 100 years to build. This castle is built on a peninsula at the edge of a lake. Others are on high ground, on the top of hills. Windows faced mainly into the inner courtyard for safety. Unwelcome visitors could not climb the walls or get in through outside windows. Castles were built to keep the enemy out, young master!"

"So that's why there aren't many windows!" mused Zentin. "Hey, that's a neat swimming pool. Do people swim in it?"

"That is a moat, Master Zentin. It goes around the castle as another form of defence. It has broken glass and sharp metal in it. I would advise any living person not to dive in," replied the knight "Come, lads! Cross the drawbridge with those soldiers and see what is inside the walls."

With their spirit forms invisible and silent to the marching soldiers, Axion, Zentin, and Sir Henry floated across the sturdy wooden planks. As they reached the other side, they saw a man turning a large wheel. Up went the drawbridge. The entrance was impenetrable.

"Wow, it's like coming into a bank vault! Hey, there's another wall inside the other wall," gasped Zentin.

"Aye, Zentin, one is the outer curtain wall, the other the inner curtain wall. If an enemy manages to get through the first wall, they shall find the inner wall impenetrable!" Sir Henry obviously had fond memories of his early childhood, living in this building.

The three spirits spent the next two hours drifting around the myriad of rooms in the castle. Sir Henry proudly showed them the castle's towers inside the inner wall. The great hall was the main living area and much activity was going on, as it was evening mealtime. The cooks' quarters were next to the kitchen. The kitchen walls were made of wood. The rest of the castle, however, was solid stone. Sir Henry explained. "The kitchen is separate from the main building to prevent any fire that might occur in the kitchen from spreading into the great hall quickly. There is also a barracks area, which houses the castle soldiers."

Zentin pointed to the swords, spears, lances and the evil-looking crossbows. "Hey, look at the old-fashioned weapons, Axion."

Sir Henry frowned. "Old fashioned? They are the newest and finest in the world, Master Zentin!"

Nearby the blacksmith was busy at work putting a new shoe onto a beautiful stallion. The horse seemed to become unsettled, flaring its nostrils when they entered. Although they were not visible, it looked as though the horse could sense that they were there in the shop!

"That is--was my horse, Lothario!" Sir Henry sighed. "They must have brought him back here to my father's castle after the battle of Bannockburn. I fear that he can sense our presence. We must leave."

"Is this the armour that Lothario had on in battle?" asked Zentin, pointing at a large section of armour, with straps and saddle, resting over a railing in the far end of the stables.

"Aye, master, it is indeed." Sir Henry sighed. He looked sad.

After they left the Blacksmith's, Axion asked, "You

miss your horse, don't you?"

"Aye, Lothario was a close friend. Knight's always had an empathy with their horses. Our horses were buried in the field behind the castle in the soft earth." He pointed to the rear wall.

"Maybe we can get Roto to beam up Lothario's ghost to you!" exclaimed Axion.

"Heck, Axion, imagine a horse ghost clopping around the space station and space ship!" Zentin laughed.

"I'll advise Sir Roto about the burial area upon our return. Perhaps it might be possible." Sir Henry looked back at the blacksmith's hut. "Come on, lads, I'll show ye the north tower," said Sir Henry, pointing to the tallest tower. Axion particularly enjoyed going up and down the spiral stones steps of the tall tower. The stairs were so narrow that only one person at a time could travel along. "Yes, the narrow passages are good for defence," explained Sir Henry. "Archers are positioned on the towers, because of their firing range and the distance they can reach from here. They fire through these special arrow holes or from the tower roof."

The castle even had its own chapel, complete with beautiful stained glass windows. The walls were seven feet thick. Some of the rooms even had window seats set into the walls. They even found some of the infamous garderobes in the north tower. They secretly observed the way the cooks prepared the food in the ancient kitchen. Delicious aromas came from the various large iron, bronze, copper, and clay pots, placed directly over the fires. A cook slowly turned a carcass skewered on a pole suspended above a fireplace. Wine and ale were also stored in the kitchen. They noted the straw on the floor. "That helps to absorb the damp," explained Sir Henry. "And the straw helps to hide the dirt brought in by the little pigs, cats and dogs that wander through the kitchen," he added.

The boys noted the draughty and cold rooms with very thick walls and high ceilings.

"It's so cold in here," stated Axion

"The fireplaces provide heat. Tapestries hanging on the wall also help keep out the cold," replied Sir Henry.

"It's dark, too! No electricity, and there aren't many windows. I know, Sir Henry," grinned Zentin, "the fewer the windows the better the defence, right?"

"Aye, but what is the electricity that ye mentioned, lad?"

"Ah, something invented in the future, Sir Henry, which provides light."

"So that is what those bright lights come from on the space ship and space station?"

"Right, Sir Henry! Hey, you learn fast!" laughed Axion.

Sir Henry blushed. "Ahem, I shall take ye to see the great hall."

"Wow! This dining room is huge!" said Zentin.

"Why are those people sitting up on a platform at the front?" asked Axion.

"They are the people who are in honourable positions in the household," replied Sir Henry.

"Look, they're throwing the bones onto the floor!" remarked Zentin.

Axion and Zentin noted the strange eating habits of the inhabitants with glee. There were no forks. Men used their own knife and spoon. "Their bowls look like stale bread," remarked Axion.

"The correct name is trenchers, Master Axion. The bread is dried, not stale," replied Sir Henry.

Axion nudged Zentin. "Yuck! They're sharing their bowls, cups, and plates! They all seem to be drinking only wine or milk or what looks like beer. Why?"

"That drink is called mead, Axion. Because the water often tastes bad, wine is preferred!" snorted Sir Henry.

"Oh, I'm sorry, Sir Henry. I didn't mean to be critical. It's just that everything is so different back in this time. I'm just interested, that's all," responded Axion.

"Me, too!" added Zentin. "Are there dungeons below?"

"Aye, I shall take ye both there."

Axion and Zentin followed along in Sir Henry's wake.

They even cruised through a solid door.

"Ace. We went straight through! Just like real ghosts!" laughed Axion.

"Yeah, this is like stepping into one of our dungeon games with the spooky castles and dungeon," giggled Zentin.

Sir Henry beamed at the boys. "Follow me lads!" He floated through another closed door and down some spiralling steps. Axion and Zentin were following so close behind him that they bumped into him when he stopped at the bottom of the stone steps. They started to shiver. There was a noise from behind one of the closed doors.

"What's that?" asked Zentin.

"Probably rats," replied Sir Henry.

"Gross! Yuck!" remarked Axion.

Their spirits went through the door to investigate. Big rats were scurrying around the straw strewn over the floor. They ran between Axion and Zentin.

"Ugh! This place gives me the creeps," said Zentin.

"I'm glad I wasn't a prisoner in the 14th Century!" Axion shivered.

"Me, too!" added Zentin, his teeth chattering. "Heck, Axion, you look as pale as a ghost!"

However, there were no prisoners in this castle dungeon, or skeletons chained to the walls, as they had seen in comic books. Sir Henry decided that it was time to leave the dungeon.

"Hey, we're running out of time, Sir Henry. Can we look at the village on the mainland next to the castle? There's only an hour left of our time here before the transporter beams us back to 3000 AD."

"Of course!" Sir Henry took them out of the castle--straight through the closed drawbridge.

"I'll never get used to going through things. Now I know what it's really like to be a ghost," squealed Axion.

Zentin laughed. "Yeah, we'd better be careful not to try and walk through doors or walls back at the space station, huh?"

The village houses had wooden supports. The spaces between these frames contained a strange material. Sir Henry explained. "This is a mixture made from mud, clay, horsehair, and the dung of animals in the area. The timber is oak from the nearby forest. Willow or oak sticks are woven together to form a type of mesh. The daub seals it and makes it waterproof."

"That's clever,' remarked Zentin.

Sir Henry continued, "The floors are dirt, covered by a layer of reeds. Some roofs are made of the woven reed and daub combination. Other roofs are made of wood. A cooking fire of peat or wood burns day and night in a clearing in the middle of the dirt floor, and the smoke then goes out through a hole in the roof called a louver."

"Heck, we're rather spoilt in 3000AD, aren't we, with air-conditioning and heating," sighed Axion. "Our houses are so comfortable!"

"Yeah, and they don't have computers or vision screens or fridges or dishwashers here," continued Zentin.

"No beds either! Well, I guess the piles of straw are their beds," added Axion.

The boys stopped, aware that Sir Henry was listening with an amused expression. "Aye, lads, ye are very spoilt!"

Outside in the fading light, they watched as a woman, oblivious to their invisible presence, balanced on a one-footed stool, and hand-milked a cow that she had tethered to a post next to her house.

"Hmm, that sure smells good. Sir Henry, I thought cows were milked by machine on the farms," remarked Axion.

"Nah, back in the olden times, back here, they didn't have machinery, Axion. Remember?" laughed Zentin.

Axion countered Zentin's last rebuff with some knowledge of his own, saying, "Look at the candles everywhere, and the fire torches hanging on the walls! A real fire danger, huh, Sir Henry?"

"Aye, unfortunately ye are correct," answered Sir Henry. There was a sudden *beep* from the communicators on Zentin and Axion's wrists. They heard Roto's familiar staccato voice.

"This is Roto. I am going to beam your spirits back to the space station in five minutes. Do you wish to stay there, Sir Henry?"

"Stay? No! Well, not at this moment. I have dedicated myself to the protection of my new masters. Now, please beam me back with Axion and Zentin, good Sir Roto. I've so much to learn in the future world. I cannot decide what to do now. Do I have to make a decision right now?"

"No, Sir Henry. Remember, the information needed to beam you back to the 14th Century is in my data base," replied Roto. "Go back to the field where you arrived and I will beam you back."

Five minutes later, the three spirits waited patiently in the field in a remote spot distant from the grazing cows. "I hope this doesn't curdle their milk!" laughed Zentin as a now familiar mist enveloped them, lifting their spirits away from the field, then started to spin into a mini tornado shape.

"Whoooooopppppppeeeeeeeee!" yelled Axion. "Away we go, back to the future!"

Seconds later, their spirits were back. They were standing in their human form on the transporter platform with Sir Henry grinning at them. "Aye, it's like coming home! I thought I would never like this magical place! Thank ye, Sir Roto. The young masters enjoyed themselves. I did too. It was grand to see my horse again. But my mother and father died years ago. I was an only child, without any heirs--the castle was to belong to the people if I died." Sir Henry paused briefly. "So ye see I really have no blood ties to my past. Could you possibly beam up Lothario's spirit from the castle? We buried our special horses in the field behind the castle."

"I can't promise anything, Sir Henry. Perhaps you may need to return and see if his ghost is still near the castle. Then I might be able to beam you both up." He turned away and said to Axion and Zentin, "If you two hurry, you will still get a few hours' sleep before breakfast." They were too tired to disagree and obediently returned to their sleeping quarters in the still silent, sleeping space station.

Sir Henry followed Roto in invisible mode to the flight deck. The flight deck crew were busy. They had spotted a space ship approaching the space station from a far off galaxy called Tarantor. The shift captain was anxious. There had been an alert issued hours earlier, warning that a rogue alien space ship with Tarantors on board, was possibly heading in their direction.

Sir Henry returned to the boy's cabin and saw their sleeping forms. *I must go back to the flight deck and see* what is happening. My new masters could be in danger from this Tarantor space ship.

Chapter 7
Aliens!

Sir Henry's invisible form was next to Roto. He listened to the voice coming through the speaker.

"This is Admiral Badun speaking from the SS Pirate. I wish to communicate with your Commander in chief, Admiral Trebor Ecurb. I demand to talk to him immediately!"

"I will have to wake the Admiral, please wait a moment."

"I'm waiting," was the reply.

The shift captain pressed the call button to Admiral Trebor's sleeping quarters. Five minutes later, Admiral Trebor Ecurb and Captain Dreamer arrived. Trebor took the microphone in his hand and pressed the button.

"Admiral Badun, this is Admiral Trebor speaking. May I ask why you have come here?"

"I must see you, Admiral Trebor Ecurb."

"To see each other in person would contravene the agreement between our planets. It was agreed, when the peace treaty was signed, that we would not trespass on each other's planets or territory, including space ships, for at least ten years. And thereafter, any visit would be a peaceful one."

There was a long silence before Badun replied. "I've come to take back my carved oak staff! It's mine! You had no right to take it from me!"

"Badun, please calm down. I don't have your staff. The day your people sentenced you to community service on Zolga, I handed the staff back to its rightful owner, King Goodun. The people had elected him to control the planet's committee, not you. I presume that you have been let out early because of your good behaviour. Why spoil everything for your family by doing something that you will regret? You're behaving like a spoilt child, instead of a mature 19 year-old! King Goodun and his committee will be forced to put you back there again."

There was another silence before Admiral Badun replied. "This is my space ship. My men will do as I command. I don't believe that you gave the staff back. I will give you 12 hours to return my carved oak staff or I will start shooting at Space Station Explorer!" Communication between the space ships went dead.

Admiral Trebor paced up and down the floor of the space station flight deck, his hands clasped behind his back. He finally stopped and turned to Captain Dreamer. "I can't let him fire on us! He'll cause great damage. Oh, he's still such an angry, immature young man. I didn't want him to go to Zolga. But that decision was up to his fellow Tarantors. This problem was the result of the Tarantors belief that a small piece of carved oak from one of Earth's oak trees is as valuable to Tarantors as one encrusted with jewels is upon Earth! Diamonds and emeralds and the like hold no value to Tarantors."

"Sir," interrupted Captain Dreamer, "what can we do? That young man is dangerous while he's like this."

"To be honest, I don't know at the moment. I don't want to take part in any hostile action, even in self-defence. It will break the treaty. Roto, do you have any ideas? There must be a solution."

Roto stood in front of his commander, busily searching his data bank. "I am sorry, Admiral, but I cannot find anything definite at the moment. I will go to my room and re-check. There's something that might work, but I need to be sure. I won't be long, sir." With that, Roto glided on his air cushions out of the area, into the transport tube and disappeared.

"I hope he's onto a solution." Admiral Trebor was worried. *"Brr,* there's that pesky little cold draft again!"

Roto did not go back to his room. Instead, he headed straight for the boys' room. He found them already up and dressed by the time he had entered. "Ah, I knew Sir Henry would be here."

The excited twins talked together, finishing each other's sentences, as was their custom.

"Roto, Sir Henry told us about the Tarantor space ship," said Axion. "He has an idea."

"A plan really, a great battle plan," continued Zentin.

"Based on his battle knowledge using a decoy," added Axion

"A diversion is needed, followed by a shock tactic. Isn't that right, Sir Henry?" Zentin asked. "Sir Henry, tell Roto your plan. It's neat!"

Roto hissed around up and down the small room and then stopped and turned towards Sir Henry, who was now visible. "Well, Sir Henry, I think we have the same idea. I was sensing your thoughts when you were up on the flight deck listening in. A decoy? A diversion? I presume you mean to use yourself as the diversion?"

"Exactly, Sir Roto. All I shall require is my horse beneath me. Lothario should be in full armour, of course. I intend to scare that young man so much that he will have second thoughts of attacking. It will be wonderful to see his face."

Axion looked puzzled. "But your horse isn't here, Sir Henry."

"Don't worry, young Axion. We have twelve hours to prepare," said Roto. He turned to Sir Henry. "With Admiral Trebor's permission to proceed, I can send you back to the 14th Century to the castle, ten years after the time you last visited. I've calculated that your horse would be dead by that time. You can go to Lothario's resting place. If luck is on our side, you may be able to communicate with his ghost. I can beam your both up when we are ready. This plan of yours may succeed, Sir Henry."

Axion suddenly sounded worried. "But, Sir Henry, you will have to show yourself to everyone. You won't be our secret anymore. You could get hurt."

"No, he can't, because he's already dead. A ghost as our champion is brilliant, Sir Henry. Awesome stuff!" gasped Zentin.

"Aye, Zentin, ye are correct. Lothario and I will be in no danger, because we are ghosts! He will love the challenge. Lothario loved to charge at the enemy in battle. Well, Sir Roto? Are ye agreed?"

"This plan is so crazy that it will work," replied Roto. "Come on, Axion and Zentin. It's time to introduce our gallant knight to your father and the people of the space station. There's no time to lose. Young Admiral Badun is getting more agitated by the hour."

"Wait, I need to adjust my armour. Where's my sword? Ah, that's it. Now, I'm ready. This time I will stay visible." *Clink! Clank! Squeak!* The bald Sir Henry, his wisps of ginger hair cascading about his shoulders, sword in its holder and helmet tucked proudly under his left arm, followed the space robot, Roto. The sandy-haired, bright-eyed twins, following in his wake, entered the transport tube. Roto pressed the button to the flight deck.

Chapter 8
Sir Henry's Quest

As the transport tube slowed to a stop at the entrance to the flight deck, Roto turned to this three excited companions, holding his mechanical hand up in a gesture of caution. "Sir Henry, Axion and Zentin, I need a quick word before I open the doors."

"What about?" asked Axion.

"Why the delay?" added Zentin.

"Please speak, Sir Roto, and we will all listen to thy noble words, fellow knight," said Sir Henry, standing as tall as he could.

Zentin sighed impatiently. "Okay, go ahead, Roto." Axion simply nodded his acknowledgment.

"I will go into the flight deck first, followed by the

twins, then Sir Henry in his current visible form. Oh, and I think you should keep your helmet off so as not to scare anyone. I'm responsible for letting you keep Sir Henry as a secret, so I think I'd better be the one to explain everything to Admiral Trebor. He's very worried now. I hope our surprise appearance and the plan we shall present to him will solve everything. Is everyone ready?"

"Yeah."

"Yep."

"Aye!"

"Right, let's go!"

Roto released the sliding doors and entered the room, instantly calling out to the Admiral to gain his attention. "Admiral, I have an important and honoured guest to introduce to you, sir."

Admiral Trebor remained with his back to the group making its entrance, shuffling papers around the centre table. "Roto? Can your guest wait? We have more pressing matters to deal with. I--huh? What's the matter, Captain Dreamer? *Brr,* there's that darn cold draft again--"

The Admiral spun around.

"Admiral, may I introduce our ghost guest?"

"A knight?" Roto, start explaining. "When did he come on board?"

The group moved across the large room. *Squeak! Clink! Clunk!* Sir Henry's proudly moved across the floor. Roto turned to Sir Henry and moved one arm in a gesture of welcome.

"Admiral Trebor Ecurb, I present to you Sir Henry de Bohun, gallant English knight, late of the 14th Century, killed at the battle of Bannockburn in Scotland, 1314 AD. He has been the honoured guest the past few days, of Axion, Zentin and myself. Admiral, Sir Henry has pledged, on his knight's code of honour, to quote *'protect the weak, defenceless and helpless, and fight for the general welfare of all'*. Sir Henry wants to defend the SS Explorer from the Tarantor rogues!" Roto then hissed back out of the way to allow Sir Henry to move across to the Admiral.

"A knight's ghost!" remarked the Admiral. "Amazing!"

Sir Henry halted, clicked his metal encased heels together, bowed his head and said in his big, booming voice, "Admiral Trebor, I am honoured to meet thee and to help in thy hour of need, sir. I am a humble knight at thy service!"

Roto said, "Admiral, I can vouch for this ghost's honesty and integrity. I can only apologise that he was not introduced earlier."

"Thank you Roto. By the way, how did you get here, Sir Henry? I suspect it wasn't by magic." Admiral Trebor looked straight at his sons, who both looked very uncomfortable indeed. "Aha! The transporter! I knew it!" he looked at his sons and added, "I'll speak to your later about this!"

"Dad, we--oh, I--hum, er." Zentin stopped.

"I told you he'd find out, Zentin. Dad always does!" remarked Axion.

Admiral Trebor then faced the ghost, saluted and then extended his right arm towards Sir Henry in an offer of a handshake. Sir Henry smiled and extending his right arm saying, "Well, good sir, methinks I may make thy hand blue with cold if I shake it."

"Brr, you're not wrong, Sir Henry," laughed Admiral Trebor in response to the icy handshake. "I can only feel the coldness. I can't physically feel you." Trebor gasped as his arm passed straight through the spirit of Sir Henry. "But I can certainly see you!"

Captain Dreamer stepped forward and saluted the knight, "Welcome aboard Space Station Explorer, Sir Henry. Thank you for your offer to help, but I can't see how--"

"Ah, good sires, with Roto's kind assistance, ye will send away that evil Badun for good! And ye will not have to put any life in any danger! My good friend, Sir Roto, has explained about the peace pact between thy people and the Tarantors. So ye see, Admiral, ye must accept this plan of defence. With Lothario, we shall scare thy enemies away and win the day without any physical violence and save thee from breaking the important treaty!"

"Who's Lothario?"

"Lothario is my horse, Admiral," replied Sir Henry.

Roto interrupted, "Admiral, we don't have much time. I need to beam up Lothario and his saddle, bridle and armour for Sir Henry as soon as possible. We shall also need to set aside one of the storage rooms to house Lothario."

"Why do you need your horse, Sir Henry?" asked Admiral Trebor.

"Sir Henry needs his horse to challenge and charge at Badun's space ship and scare him away, back to his own galaxy," replied Roto.

"But, Sir Henry and Lothario will be killed. Badun will use his weapons. Hold on, what am I saying? You can't be killed; you're already dead! I say--by heck, this idea is so crazy that it could work--however, I need to consider it."

Roto responded, "Admiral, please trust me and Sir Henry, this plan will work. No physical confrontation will be used, so the treaty is safe. I've already checked the positives and negatives. It will work."

The Admiral smiled. "Thank you, Roto. I'll agree to

the plan, as you've obviously considered everything. I trust your judgement as you've helped us before in such situations."

Everyone was suddenly silent as the engineer called out, "Sir, we have contact from Admiral Badun! He wants to speak to you immediately."

Admiral Trebor rushed to the viewing screen, which had popped up from the flight deck console. Admiral Badun's voice crackled over the intercom. "Trebor, you now have only six hours left."

Admiral Trebor looked at Badun's image on the screen. A strange-looking face, greenish coloured, with pointed pixie-like ears, a flat nose and two large, orange eyes, stared at them from the space station's monitor screen.

"Badun, I'm fully aware of that fact. I shall contact you before your deadline."

"I'm going to enjoy this! I'll wait for your contact then." The communication was again stopped by the Tarantors.

Admiral Trebor sighed and pressed the button, which returned the viewing screen out of sight. He looked at Sir Henry de Bohun. "It's such a pity that the old king and queen of the planet Tarantor produced twin sons of such opposite character. The older twin is a wise king and his people are happy. A year ago, I was the chairperson at a meeting to decide the king's brother's punishment. It was an intergalactic meeting, with many planets represented. Badun had become too much of a nuisance, whizzing around space with his gang of followers, causing havoc wherever he went. He had fired laser beams dangerously close to other space ships. In the end it was decided to ban him from flying and that he should do a year of community service and rehabilitation, in the hope that he might become a good Tarantor citizen."

"That punishment has obviously not succeeded, Admiral," replied Sir Henry, shaking his head. "In my time, he would have been executed!"

"The intergalactic law does not believe in an *eye for an eye* or punitive punishment, Sir Henry. We try to reform them," stated Roto.

Trebor smiled at Sir Henry. "Well, good sir, it's time I let Roto and the engineer organize your trip back in time to find the spirit of your horse, Lothario. I'm sure you'll find him, and Roto can beam you both back to us. I'm going to enjoy your encounter with this mischief-maker! I still find it hard to believe that I'm talking to a ghost myself!"

Chapter 9
The Knight in Space

Ten minutes later, Sir Henry peered at the flashing lights and bouncing dials on the space station's transporter console. This transporter room was much larger than the small one he had first encountered.

"Are ye sure that we can find Lothario's spirit, Sir Roto? It has been such a long time. I wonder if he will recognize me!"

"Sir Henry, please don't worry so. I have all the coordinates from my database. Besides, the boys told me that Lothario had become anxious when you visited his stable. I'm sure he could sense your presence. Relax, good knight. Here's a communicator for your wrist. Let the transporter do its work." Roto put the communicator around sir Henry's left wrist.

"Thank ye, Sir Roto. I am ready to go," said Sir Henry.

"I'll now beam you back to the field where you say all the knight's horses were buried. Let me know when you have found Lothario. We're also going to beam up a saddle, bridle and, of course, head armour, for Lothario. You will make an awesome sight!" Roto and the engineer pressed more buttons, then stood back and waited in silence. Mist started to form in the dome covering the transporter platform. Within seconds, Sir Henry had disappeared.

"I hope he finds Lothario's spirit," added Axion.

"I hope so, too," responded Roto. "We have exactly 5 hours left before the encounter."

Ten minutes passed.

"Has he disappeared for good?" asked Axion.

"No, Master Axion, I still have contact with his spirit-- Aha, I now have contact with two forms."

Sir Henry's voice echoed through the transporter room. "Sir Roto, I've found him! Thank God, I've found his spirit. It's as if we've never been apart. I told ye we had a close bond. You've made me a happy man." The noise of a horse could be heard. "Time to beam us up, Sir Roto."

"Your wish is my command, Sir Henry," responded

Roto. He pressed some buttons and mist formed in the transporter dome. A few seconds and the mists cleared. Sir Henry appeared, standing proudly next to the magnificent stallion's ghost and all the battle armour for the horse. Sir Henry looked at the equipment on the platform and gasped.

"Oh, thank ye, Sir Roto. What a nice surprise!"

Roto had also beamed up Sir Henry's prized lance, complete with its standard, or flag, in the matching gold and blue of the material of the Lothario's caparison, or war coat.

"Oh, ye are indeed a wonderful knight, Sir Roto. Well done! My lance will be a perfect weapon!" Sir Henry swooped on the equipment.

Axion and Zentin stood watching, open-mouthed. The horse caparison matched the surcoat, or over coat, that Sir Henry was wearing over his armour. They were unable to assist the knight as he collected the equipment bridle and saddle, because they couldn't feel any of the items.

Lothario only had eyes for his beloved master, Sir Henry de Bohun. He pranced around like a young colt. He finally calmed down as Sir Henry whispered into his ear, giving him a pat on his nose as he put on the bridle.

There were tears in Sir Henry's eyes when he turned around. "Thank ye, one and all! Ye have made me a very happy man--err, ghost!" he grinned. "Aye, and Lothario is obviously delighted to be with me again. He does not appear to be a year older than the last time we rode together when I charged at that rascal King Robert the Bruce."

Trebor cleared his throat and stuttered, "K-King Robert the B-Bruce--I--oh, never mind, Sir Henry. I'll talk to you later about that--"

"Well, Sir Henry," interrupted Roto hastily, "I checked back through my history data bank, and I found that Lothario only lived a few months after you were killed. It was recorded on his grave that he had died of a broken heart. No wonder he's pleased to see you again!"

Everyone laughed. Then Admiral Trebor said, "Well, Sir Henry, we shall let Roto and the boys help you get ready for the tournament. Please come to the flight deck when you're ready. At least a ghost of a horse can't damage anything! We only have four hours left, and I don't wish to let Badun get angrier than he already is. I know Roto has told you about the lasers. I must go back to the flight deck now."

"Aye, that he has, Admiral. Lothario is afraid of nothing, so do not fear for us. I know the beams will not hurt us! We shall be ready for battle in an hour."

"Good. I look forward to seeing you in full tournament dress, Sir Henry." The Admiral departed through the travel tube.

The twins watched, fascinated, as Sir Henry put on the crinet and chanfrom, which protected Lothario's neck. The caparison was put over Lothario's back and the straps buckled across his chest and around his strong neck. Finally, the saddle was put on. Axion and Zentin put a box next to Lothario so that Sir Henry could step up and pull himself up onto Lothario's back. "Well, young masters, what do ye think?"

"Fantastic!"

"Fearsome!"

"Go, Sir Henry!" added the engineer.

By the time Axion, Zentin, Roto and the engineer arrived back at the flight deck, Sir Henry and Lothario had already arrived. They were standing in full splendour in the middle of the room with the flight crew passing appreciative comments.

"Are you ready, Sir Henry?" asked Admiral Trebor.

"Aye!"

"Right! Stay out here out of sight, while I commence the plan. Captain Dreamer, get Admiral Badun on the communicator please."

"Yes, sir!"

The screen appeared from the consul, startling Lothario, who moved backwards a few paces.

"Admiral Badun, our champion is ready to meet you in

space!"

"This will be fun! Fancy sending out only one solitary soul to challenge us! Go ahead, send the poor fool out!" replied Badun. He then disappeared from the screen.

"Fool indeed!" snorted Sir Henry. "We shall see who the real fool is shortly" Sir Henry put on his helmet and placed the lance in its holder. "Do not worry, sire! Enjoy the joust!" With that comment, Sir Henry rode Lothario out through the walls of the flight deck, down to the docking area where the docking crew had opened the wide doors especially for Sir Henry's grand entrance into space. Admiral Trebor had chosen the docking area so that Badun could not see that Sir Henry was a ghost who could walk through walls. It was all part of Sir Henry's plan.

Everyone in the space station peered out through the nearest windows to watch the spectacle of the 14th Century clashing with the 31st Century. As Sir Henry rode out through the doors, Admiral Trebor ordered the invisible, protective shield be put on to protect the station against any stray laser beam.

Everyone on the flight deck of Badun's ship stared at the magnificent sight standing in full tournament dress in front of his hovering space ship.

"It's a knight in armour astride a horse! This is going to be so easy. Ha! He's starting to charge at us. The silly fool! Well, maybe he's a brave fool! Charge back at him! Fire the laser! Wha--what's happened? Where is he? Where did he go?"

Sir Henry made himself visible again. He noted that Badun's greenish face had turned a pale shade of lemon. His eyes bulged in terror as the flashing light of the laser sparkled from the knight's armour like a dazzling display of fireworks.

Badun shouted, "The laser went right through him! He's coming straight at us again. We're going to crash ... *No! No! No!*"

The other Tarantors ducked for cover as Sir Henry, on Lothario, galloped straight at the front windshield, his lance now out of its holder and pointed at them. The spirits charged right through the windshield and through the terrified Tarantors, then out through the back of the spacecraft. An eerie silence and icy breeze enveloped the Tarantors. Sir Henry grinned as a now pasty-lemon coloured Badun nervously poked his head up over the instrument panel.

Lothario reared up as Sir Henry, seated upright, held his lance up in victory, the standard flapping in space as he moved it from side to side. It was as Roto said later, "Indeed, a sight to behold."

Sir Henry sat up straight and proud in the saddle as he spoke. "Admiral Badun, I declare a victory! Ye must go straight back to Tarantor. That is my master's wish. Thy brother is awaiting thy arrival. If I hear that ye have not mended thy ways, I shall visit Planet Tarantor and deal with thee directly!"

Badun replied, "Sir Henry, we are going. I don't know what sort of powers you have, but I'm not staying to find out." He turned to his crew and shouted, "Get us out of here, before Admiral Trebor lets Sir Henry loose again."

Sir Henry waited until the space ship had disappeared from his sight before returning to the Space Station, to acknowledge the cheering and clapping inhabitants. The proudest of all were Axion and Zentin.

Chapter 10
The Knight's Wish

There were great celebrations that evening. Sir Henry was the guest of honour, and of course, Lothario was standing next to his beloved master, as Admiral Trebor cleared his throat to make a speech.

"Ladies and gentlemen, may I have your attention for a few moments, please? Thank you. I'd like to propose a toast to Sir Henry and, of course, to his beautiful horse, Lothario. I believe that every child here has asked Sir Henry if they can have a ride. I believe Sir Henry has now discovered that he and Lothario can turn into a more solid form, so maybe these rides will be possible."

Yay! Hooray!

"We are celebrating two things tonight. First, we have

repelled the menace of a rather confused and, may I say, now repentant Badun. His brother, King Goodun, has advised me, just before this celebration, that his brother has arrived back at the Planet Taranto and is now back in detention to undergo further rehabilitation counselling. King Goodun did say that his brother kept repeating that we Earthlings had discovered a new magical kind of super man! I'd like to be more accurate and say we have a super knight!" The admiral paused when everyone started to clap. "Sir Henry came to us by chance, beamed up accidentally from the 14th century-- 1314, to be precise, during the battle of Bannockburn-- shortly after his enemy, Robert Bruce, Earl of Carrick, King of Scotland, had confronted his charge and killed him with his axe." Sir Henry nodded in agreement. The Admiral continued, "I advised Sir Henry earlier this evening, that his wish would be our command! He told me that he would reveal his wish to this gathering tonight. But first, I'd like everyone here to raise their glass in a toast to our gallant knight, Sir Henry de Bohun."

Cheers! Well-done, Sir Henry!

Admiral Trebor left the podium and started clapping as Sir Henry reluctantly, but proudly, took his place in front of the admiring audience.

"Being spirited to the future is an incredible

experience. May I say I like the fact that at last Earth and what ye call space, with its myriad of galaxies, are at peace. Sadly, I did not see peace in my time! I am both pleased and proud that ye have learned something from history. For the first time, I feel at peace. I no longer believe in war or conflict and shall strive to keep peace in the future."

Well spoken!

What's your wish?

"Aye, my wish! At first, I pondered upon returning to the past. But I would be a ghost! Here in the future, I am still a ghost, but a happy ghost. Not only with the company of my faithful Lothario, but also newfound friends, especially Axion and Zentin and my fellow modern knight, Sir Roto. My wish is to stay here, with my horse Lothario. I wish to remain thy faithful knight, Admiral. I shall keep the knight's code of honour: 'To defend the weak, be courteous to all women, be loyal to my master, serve God at all times, and give mercy to a vanquished enemy.' I am thy humble servant." Sir Henry then dropped to one knee in front of Admiral Trebor Ecurb.

Everyone present stood up, clapped and cheered in unison. It was some moments before Admiral Trebor could make himself heard.

"Please stand, Sir Henry! Your wish is my command.

Welcome to our community!"

Axion and Zentin were the first to rush forward to hug the Gallant Knight's chilly but happy spirit.

"Sir Henry, I'm glad you chose to stay," said Axion.

Zentin said, "Sir Henry, Dad told us that our surname Ecurb was changed generations ago by one of our ancestors. It's the reverse of Bruce. Dad's name Trebor is the reverse of--"

Sir Henry laughed. "I know, Robert Bruce. He told me just after the joust. Strange is it not, that I am now a friend of Robert the Bruce's family and protecting his descendants!"

The End

**You can find ALL our books
up on our website at:**
http://www.writers-exchange.com

All Wendy's Books:
http://www.writers-exchange.com/Wendy-Laing/

All our Mid-Grade Readers:
*https://www.writers-
exchange.com/category/genres/children/mid-grade-
primary/*

About the Author

Wendy **Laing** is one half of the pseudonym or pen name "Dalziel Laing" of Dianne Dalziel and Wendy Laing, the co-authors of *Mirror, Mirror.* She is also a multi-published author in her own right.

In retirement, a writer, with a Teaching Diploma, a Bachelor of Arts Degree with majors in professional Writing (creative writing editing, publishing and Journalism) and Communications (mass media, and gender imaging) with electives in Literary Studies and Sociology, and Master of Arts (project/thesis called: "Severance Packages, A crime/Paranormal Novel and

Exegesis focussing on the electronic and Digital publication of Creative Writing".

A "Jill-Of-All-Trades" Teacher, curriculum consultant, travel consultant, International Airline employee in passenger and cargo areas at Melbourne International Airport and city offices, and a Professional Dog Trainer! Wendy's had articles published in *The Sunbury Times* and *The Anthony Warlow International Newsletter.*

Member of the FAW (Fellowship of Australian Writers)
Member of the VWC (Victorian Writers Centre)
Lifetime Alumni of Victoria University
Member of Sister in Crime

Widowed in 2016, Wendy lives in a retirement village with her four pawed family, Vicky, a sooky & loving adopted black Greyhound, whom she has trained and takes to Pet therapy at the local aged care each week - a hobby that she has enjoyed for over 30 years.

Keep track of Wendy's many books on her author page:
http://www.writers-exchange.com/Wendy-Laing/

If you enjoyed this author's book, then please place a review up at the site of purchase, and any social media sites you frequent!

If you want to read more about books by this author, they are listed on the following pages...

Captain Angus, the Lighthouse Ghost

{Mid-Grade Reader: Paranormal}

Two children holidaying at the Cape Otway Lighthouse Station in Victoria Australia meet the ghost of an old Scottish sea captain who roams the world helping the 'spirits' of lighthouses and helping 'conserve' the towers. Captain Angus befriends the children and takes them on virtual reality trips via a magic time tunnel. Together, they experience sailing on an old sailor's vessel, see a shipwreck rescue, witness the tower being built, and even meet one of their own ancestors!

Publisher: http://www.writers-exchange.com/Captain-Angus-the-Lighthouse-Ghost/

Cock of the Walk

{Murder Mystery}

When Sir Peter Percival, owner of the Woodburne Wine Estate and former member of Parliament, is found dead, three Australian detectives embark on a baffling investigation in which it appears *everyone* has a motive...

Publisher: http://www.writers-exchange.com/Cock-of-the-Walk/

Sir Henry, the Knight in Space

{Science Fiction/Mid-Grade Reader}

Twin boys accidentally beam the ghost of 14th century Sir Henry de Bohun into their father's spaceship in 3000 AD. Let the fun begin as they take a virtual trip back in time to visit Sir Henry's English castle!

Publisher: http://www.writers-exchange.com/Sir-Henry-the-Knight-In-Space/

Jane Doe Mystery Series
{Mystery/Paranormal}

As the daughter of a policeman who died in the line of duty, Inspector Jane Doe, head of Melbourne Homicide, is single-mindedly driven to seek justice for all. But Jane is no ordinary detective. She can communicate with the ghosts of murder victims. Not wanting to be dismissed as mentally unstable, she must keep her secret from all but her husband and her senior officer, using each victim's information to subtly direct her team in the right direction on each case. Jane realizes she's the only thing standing between a killer being brought to justice and a monster getting off scot-free. But, with each case she solves, her fear that the police hierarchy will accidentally discover her secret forces her to walk a fine line indeed.

Book 1: Flowers from the Grave

Recovering from near fatal head injuries received from a serial killer, who is still at large, Inspector Jane Doe, head of Melbourne Homicide, is staying in an isolated clifftop cottage. Ryan, a stranger on the beach, befriends her. But Jane's idyllic sojourn turns into a nightmare. Flowers arrive with threatening notes attached. Worse, she can't help but believe that Ryan is some kind of ghost, and, if he is, is he friend or foe? Has the serial killer she apprehended in the name of justice returned to finish what he started and make her his next victim?

Publisher: http://www.writers-exchange.com/Flowers-From-The-Grave/

Book 2: Severance Packages

Set in the peaceful town of Sunbury, Australia, Inspector Jane Doe, head of Melbourne Homicide, once again deals with a serial killer after grisly, dismembered body parts are discovered at a local winery and the rubbish dump. Jane has to act fast to stop any more of these 'severance packages' from being delivered.

Publisher: http://www.writers-exchange.com/Severance-Packages/

Book 3: Haunted Heart

Head of Melbourne Homicide, Inspector Jane Doe's first Cold Case involves the recent death of a daughter of a Member of Parliament. After he disagrees with the first coroner's verdict of accidental death, the MP secures a second autopsy that reveals his daughter was murdered. At the same time, Jane's husband Oliver is dealing with a young heart transplant recipient who's having nightmares of being murdered. Elsewhere, another law enforcement officer, Steve Ho, investigates the murder

of an eminent heart transplant surgeon found in a local lake. Jane, Oliver and Steve become embroiled in a case that will surely haunt them all for years to come.
Publisher: http://www.writers-exchange.com/Haunted-Heart/

Book 4: Cadavers' Cave

Chief Superintendent of the Cold Case Squad, Jane Doe has a formidable list of special, unsolved cases littering her desk. Taking a break is a luxury she doesn't often allow herself. However, during a rare weekend off, she catches a news story involving a dead body wrapped in a plastic shroud. The gruesome discovery was made in the cliffs below the Point Lonsdale Lighthouse--directly near the entrance to the Port Phillip Bay in Victoria, Australia. Rough winter weather combined with unusually heavy, high tides washed away the grave, leaving it partially covered in rocks and seaweed. The coroner estimates that the body had been buried there for at least a year. The last thing Jane needs is another case to hit her already groaning desk, but something eerie took place in Cadavers' Cave and she may be the only one who can solve a mystery equally troubling and tragic.
Publisher: http://www.writers-exchange.com/Cadavers-Cave/

Book 5: The Ghostly Gum

Detective Chief Superintendent Jane Doe has a formidable list of cold cases on her desk. This latest one involves an unidentified person, murdered seventeen years earlier.

It is not only a perplexing case, but also an exploratory challenge for all involved as the squad try not only to identify the victim, but sort out suspects who are involved in money laundering, drugs and family feuds.

Jane's team are challenged to find solid forensic proof to use against the main suspect, so he doesn't get away with a cold-blooded murder.

Publisher: http://www.writers-exchange.com/The-Ghostly-Gum/

Mind's Eye-The imagery of remembered scenes

{Poetry}

A collection of poems encompassing one life filled with images from childhood, family, pets, the Australian countryside around, and delivered with a touch of homespun philosophy.

Publisher: http://www.writers-exchange.com/Minds-Eye/

Under the Coolabah Tree

{A Collection of Australian Poetry}

Fun, amusing, sometimes rowdy and always delightfully full of Australian colour, this collection of Australian Bush poems is best read out loud--if you dare to try an Aussie accent!

Publisher: http://www.writers-exchange.com/Under-the-Coolabah-Tree/

Mirror, Mirror
with Di Dalziel (writing as Dalziel Laing)

{Murder Mystery}

Inspector Georgina Borg's life is an emotional rollercoaster. She's deeply in love with Professor Richard Thompson yet can't get herself to commit to a permanent relationship--a puzzle even she can't explain adequately. At work, she's in charge of a case pursuing a serial killer who's remained a mystery for ten long years. She's followed his distinctive but maddeningly elusive trail from Sydney to Melbourne. Now suddenly the killer targets a victim with an entirely new profile. Despite the change in modus operandi, Borg is certain it's the same killer. Just when she thinks she's close to solving the puzzle and revealing his identity at last, her should-be, would-be fiancé becomes the prime suspect!

Publisher: http://www.writers-exchange.com/Mirror-Mirror/

Tarmac Tales
By Wendy and Dave Laing

In this fact-based collection of experiences in the airline and travel industries gathered by authors with a combined fifty-two years working in all capacities of the business, you'll be given a behind-the-scenes look at the inner operations of this sometimes funny, sometimes sad, but always entertaining trade.

Publisher: http://www.writers-exchange.com/Tarmac-Tales/

www.ingramcontent.com/pod-product-compliance
Lightning Source LLC
Chambersburg PA
CBHW071341130726
47996CB00002B/804